My Grandma, the Rock Star

Amelia Fitch

Illustrated by Kevin Burgemeestre

Rigby

Contents

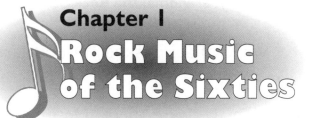

Chapter 1
Rock Music of the Sixties

"**W**ell, look at that!" said Grandpa.

We all stopped what we were doing and looked at him. My older brother Toby and I stopped eating our breakfast. Dad stopped putting on his work boots. Mom stopped spooning cereal into our baby sister, Belinda. Grandma stopped packing her briefcase with one hand and pouring juice with the other. We all waited. But Grandpa just kept on reading the newspaper.

"Well, what?" asked Dad, at last.

Grandpa looked up, as if he'd forgotten we were there. He rattled the newspaper. "Oh, there's a rock concert coming to town," he said. "Rock music of the sixties. They've got all the original bands together again."

We all went back to what we'd been doing. We weren't really into rock music from the sixties. Only Grandma was still interested. She leaned over Grandpa's shoulder and looked at the newspaper for herself.

"Oh, yes!" she said. "I remember all those groups."

"Funny to think they're still performing," said Mom. She popped another spoonful of cereal into Belinda's open mouth.

Grandma pretended to be offended.

"Well, they're the same age as your father and me," she said. "Of course they're still performing! Why wouldn't they be?"

Grandpa wasn't listening. He was still reading the paper. "And look at this!" he said.

"What?" asked Dad again.

"One of the rock groups is the Travelers!" Grandpa looked up at Grandma. "That's the group you used to sing with, isn't it, Jen? Before they went overseas and got famous?"

This time we were all interested. We knew Grandma had sung with a rock group when she was young, but we'd never thought that group would still be playing.

Toby and I grinned at each other. It always seemed funny to us, to think our grandma was once in a rock group.

Grandma took the newspaper from Grandpa. "The Travelers! Yes, that's them," she said. "Imagine! And look, there's a picture. The very same people." She laughed. "Well, they all look a bit older. But then, I suppose I do, too."

Mom smiled at her. "You look great, Mom!" she said.

"Oh, sure," said Grandma. She looked at the clock. "Oh, no! I've got to get to school! Come on, Sam and Toby. Brush your teeth and go out to the car!"

We always drive to school with Grandma. She works at our school. In fact, she's the principal of our school.

"Beat you to the bathroom, Sam!" said Toby. He always likes to be first.

But this morning, I didn't try to race him. I wanted to ask Grandma something. Toby ran off down the hall.

Then I said, "Why didn't you go overseas with the Travelers and get famous, too, Grandma?"

Grandma smiled at Grandpa. "Oh, I had my reasons, Sam," she said. Grandpa smiled back at her.

"For one thing, Grandma wanted to be a teacher," said Mom. "She couldn't have done that if she'd gone with the Travelers."

"You wanted to be a teacher more than you wanted to be a rock star?" I asked. "I can't believe that!"

"Sometimes I can't believe it myself," said Grandma, "especially when I can't get you kids into the car in the morning. Move it, Sam!"

I thought about Grandma and the Travelers all that day. That evening, I got the newspaper and looked for the advertisement Grandpa had seen.

"What are you looking for?" asked Toby.

I'd found the advertisement by then. "This," I said.

Toby looked. "Oh, that corny sixties rock concert," he said. "What are you looking at that for?"

"Well, I thought maybe Grandpa could take Grandma to the concert," I said.

Dad came into the room. "That's a good idea," he said. "Grandma'd love that!" He took the paper from me and looked at it. "In fact, why don't we all go? Sounds like fun. And Grandma'd like it if we all went."

"You can count me out," Toby said. "Sixties music? Yuck!"

"Oh, I think we might count you in," said Dad. "It's a great idea! I'll see if we can get tickets." He left with the paper.

Toby glared at me. "Why can't you keep your big ideas to yourself?"

Later that evening, I could hear Grandma singing Belinda to sleep. She often does that. I like to listen.

Grandma sings lots of different songs. But there's one special one that she sings. It's a song about a train, and a girl leaving on it, and she's saying goodbye to someone who's staying behind. It's a sad song, but it's Belinda's favorite.

When I heard Grandma's special song drifting from Belinda's room, I stopped doing my homework and listened. Grandpa saw me listening.

"That's one of my favorites, too," he said. "It's one of the songs your grandma used to sing when she was in the Travelers."

Grandpa got up and walked to the bookshelf. "In fact," he said, "I might be able to find an old picture."

Grandpa came back with an old photo album in his hand. "There you are," he said. "That's what your grandma looked like when I first knew her."

Toby and I leaned over the album. "Wow! That's *Grandma*?" we asked.

"Sure is," said Grandpa. "I thought that'd surprise you!"

He was right. The picture must have been taken at a concert. There was a group playing guitars, drums, and a keyboard. In the front was a girl with long, blond hair, right down to her waist, and a dress with a skirt right up past her knees. She held a tambourine, and she was smiling. She looked great—but she didn't look much like our grandma.

Dad and Mom looked, too. "You look a lot like her," said Dad to Mom.

"I wish!" said Mom. "I never had hair like that!"

Toby and I just stared. It was a whole new way of thinking about our grandma. "Do you think Grandma would let us take the picture to school and show the kids?" I asked.

Mom, Dad, and Grandpa laughed. "Not a chance!" they said.

Chapter 3

Blast from the Past

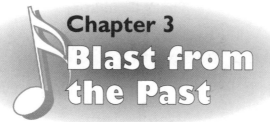

A few weeks went by. The concert was just two days away. Dad had tickets for all of us—even Belinda. *And* Toby, although Toby wasn't very pleased about it. He thought it was going to be corny.

Then, as we watched the news on TV one night, the announcer said, "Here's a blast from the past! Bands began arriving in town today for the "Return to the Sixties" rock concert. Our reporter caught up with one of the bands—a local group who went overseas and made good! Here's her interview with the Travelers!"

We all sat straight up and stared. Grandpa turned up the volume on the TV.

The interview was all about the Travelers' hit songs, and how they'd started out right in our town. Then they went overseas and became famous. This was the first time they'd ever been back to their old town. The interview ended by showing the Travelers walking into a big hotel in town and waving to the crowds who'd come to see them.

"Well!" said Grandma. "Fancy that! I have to say, it was nice to see them all again."

"Why don't you call them at the hotel, Grandma?" I asked. "You know where they're staying."

"Call them?" asked Grandma. "Oh, I don't think so."

"Why not?" asked Grandpa.

"Why not?" asked Mom. "They'd probably love to hear from you."

"If they even remember me," said Grandma.

"Of course they'll remember you!" I said. "Go on, Grandma!"

"Well," said Grandma, "it would be nice to talk to them after all this time. Should I?"

"Yes!" we all said.

I rushed to the phone book and flipped through the pages. "Here's the hotel's number!" I said.

Grandma went to the phone. She dialed. We all waited.

"Yes, hello," she said. "I wonder if I could speak to the Travelers, please?" She listened for a moment.

"Oh," she said. "Oh, I see. Then, could I leave a message? Tell them that Jennifer Carmody called." She gave our phone number to the person on the other end of the phone.

Grandma put the phone down slowly and turned to face us. "The hotel said they've been told not to put calls through to any of the bands," she said. "But they'll take messages for them."

"Never mind," said Mom. "The Travelers will call you back as soon as they get the message."

But they didn't.

Chapter 4

Still No Reply

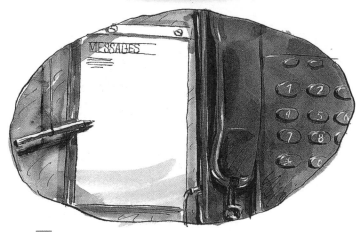

There was no call from the Travelers that night. Or the next morning, either.

When Grandma, Toby, and I got back from school in the afternoon, I saw Grandma look at the pad by the phone where we write all the messages. But there had been no call from the Travelers during the day.

"Call again, Grandma," I said.

"Maybe they didn't get the message."

"Well, all right," said Grandma. "Maybe they didn't."

So Grandma called the hotel again. "Yes," she said, "that's right. Jennifer Carmody. I did leave a message." She put the phone down. "The hotel said all messages had been given out," she said. "Well, we'll see if they call back tonight."

But they didn't.

By eight o'clock, when I had to go to bed, there had been no phone calls at all.

"That's it, then," said Grandma. "They're not going to call. I suppose they've forgotten all about me."

We didn't know what to say. Grandma looked upset.

"Those Travelers have gotten too big for their boots!" growled Grandpa.

"Goodness, it doesn't matter," said Grandma. "No big deal!" But she still looked a bit sad.

I gave her a hug. "Who needs them anyway?" I asked. Grandma hugged me back.

When the night of the concert arrived at last, Grandma didn't seem very excited about going. She'd told us it didn't matter one bit that the Travelers hadn't called, but I thought she did mind, really.

When the rest of us were all ready to go, Grandma still wasn't dressed.

"You know, I don't know whether I'll bother going," she said. "I'm a little tired. Maybe I'll stay at home."

"Cool!" said Toby. "Can I stay home, too?"

Dad gave Toby a look. We all turned to Grandma.

"Oh, Mom!"

"Oh, Jen!"

"Oh, Grandma!" we said.

Grandma saw our faces. She got up from her chair. "On second thought, of course I'll come," she said. "Give me five minutes to get ready."

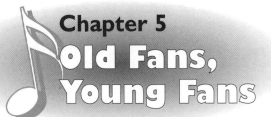

Chapter 5
Old Fans, Young Fans

We couldn't believe the crowds outside the concert hall. There were people everywhere. Most of them were around Grandma and Grandpa's age. They'd come to hear all the groups they'd liked when they were young.

"They'd nearly *all* have to be grandparents now," I thought. There weren't very many people Mom and Dad's age, and there were hardly any kids.

Toby kept his cap pulled down over his face. "It's embarrassing!" he said. "Imagine going to a sixties concert! I hope no one I know sees me!"

"They might," I said. "There's a TV news team here."

"Oh, no!" said Toby. "Where?"

"Right behind you," I said.

Before Toby could turn around, the TV reporter had spotted us. She came up and held a microphone in front of Toby. "Here's a young fan of sixties music!" she said. "Would you like to tell us about your favorite group?"

"No way!" said Toby. He disappeared behind Dad.

Dad and the reporter looked at each other and shrugged their shoulders. "Shy, is he?" asked the reporter.

"Not as a rule," said Dad.

So the reporter got the camera operator to film Belinda instead. "This would have to be the very youngest fan here!" she said.

We went in and found our seats. The concert hall was full. Everyone looked happy and excited. All those grandparents looked as if they meant to have a wonderful time.

And they did.

So did I. I'd never known sixties music could be so much fun. I knew a lot of the songs. The audience got right into it—they clapped, they sang, and a few even got up and danced in the aisles when their favorite bands came on stage.

As each band went off stage, the crowd cheered them. They were having a ball. So were Grandma and Grandpa, and Mom and Dad. Belinda was bouncing up and down on Mom's knee. Even Toby looked as if he was having a good time.

Then the Travelers came on stage.

The Travelers waved to the audience and arranged their instruments. When they were almost ready, the leader came to the front of the stage. He held up his hand to quiet the audience. He looked as if he wanted to say something.

"Before we start, I'd like to say something," the leader said. "You know, the Travelers started out in this town quite a few years ago. And then we went overseas. But when we left, one of the original Travelers didn't go with us. And that person's been trying to get in touch with us over the last few days. But we didn't get the messages until just a few minutes ago."

He stopped and peered out into the audience. "We'd really like to see that

person and we're so sorry we didn't get the messages. So we just wondered if that person might be here tonight. Jen? Jennifer Carmody? Are you in the audience?" the leader asked.

Grandma didn't move. She didn't say anything.

The audience all looked around, wondering if the person he was asking for was there. Mom, Dad, and Grandpa all looked at Grandma. Grandma still didn't move.

"Grandma, he's talking to you!" Toby and I hissed.

"Are you in the audience, Jen Carmody?" the leader asked again.

Toby and I leaped to our feet. "Yes!" we yelled. "Yes, she is!" We grabbed Grandma's hands and pulled her to her feet.

The whole audience turned to look. Some of them started to clap.

"Oh, dear," said Grandma.

"Go on, Mom!" said our mom.

"Jen!" shouted the man on the stage. "Oh, Jen! Come on up here!"

"I don't think . . ." said Grandma.

Toby and I grabbed Grandma's hands again and dragged her to the steps that led to the stage.

The leader ran down. "Thanks!" he said to us. He gave Grandma a big hug.

"Oh, Jen!" he said. Then he led her up onto the stage.

"Ladies and gentlemen, this is Jennifer Carmody," he said. "One of the original members of the Travelers! Jen chose not to go overseas with us— she had other things to do . . ."

He looked at Toby and me. "This is the result, eh, Jen?"

Grandma laughed. "Part of it," she said.

"Tonight," the man said, "tonight, the Travelers are all together again! And we'd like it—we'd love it—if Jen would join us in a song."

He looked at Grandma. "There was one song we used to do—a special song—a song that was so much Jen's song that we never played it again after she left us. But we'd like to do it tonight. Would you, Jen?"

"I'd be delighted," said Grandma.

The man bowed to her and gave her the microphone.

Toby and I made our way back to our seats. Mom smiled at me. "I think I know what song it's going to be," I whispered.

Mom nodded. "So do I," she said.

Chapter 7

Famous at Last

And I was right. As soon as the music started, Belinda knew, too. She'd been almost asleep, curled up on Mom's knee. Now, she sat straight up.

"Train song!" she said.

"Yes, darling," said Mom. "The train song."

The lights went dim. There was just one bright light, right on Grandma. I'd never heard a group play the music for Grandma's train song before. I'd only heard her sing the song by herself. With the music, the song was even better. It was still sad—but it was beautiful.

The music filled the whole hall. The audience was very quiet. Almost at the end of the song, the group stopped playing and Grandma's voice went on by itself. Then it died away.

The song was over.

Grandma stood very still on the stage. All the people in the audience were totally silent. Then they clapped and clapped and clapped. It was ages before Grandma could leave the Travelers and come back to us.

The next morning, the newspaper had a big picture of Grandma and the Travelers, right on the front page. The kids at school were totally flipped.

"It's our principal!" they said. "It's Ms. Alberti! It can't be!"

"Yes, it is," Toby and I said. "She used to be a big rock star, you know."

"Wow!" the kids said. "Cool!"

Then one of them said, "But the paper says "rejoins the Travelers." Does that mean Ms. Alberti's going to leave? Is she going back to her job with the band?"

"No!" said Toby and I. "Why would she do that? She doesn't need a job. She's already got a job. She's our grandma."